Quick as a Cricket

by Audrey Wood

illustrated by Don Wood

Published by Child's Play (International) Ltd

© M Twinn 1982   ISBN 0-85953-151-1 (hard cover)   Printed in China
This impression 1998   ISBN 0-85953-306-9 (soft cover)
Library of Congress Catalogue Number 90-46413
A catalogue reference for this book is available from the British Library.

I'm as quick as a cricket,

I'm as slow as a snail,

I'm as small as an ant,

I'm as large as a whale.

I'm as sad as a basset,

I'm as happy as a lark,

I'm as nice as a bunny,

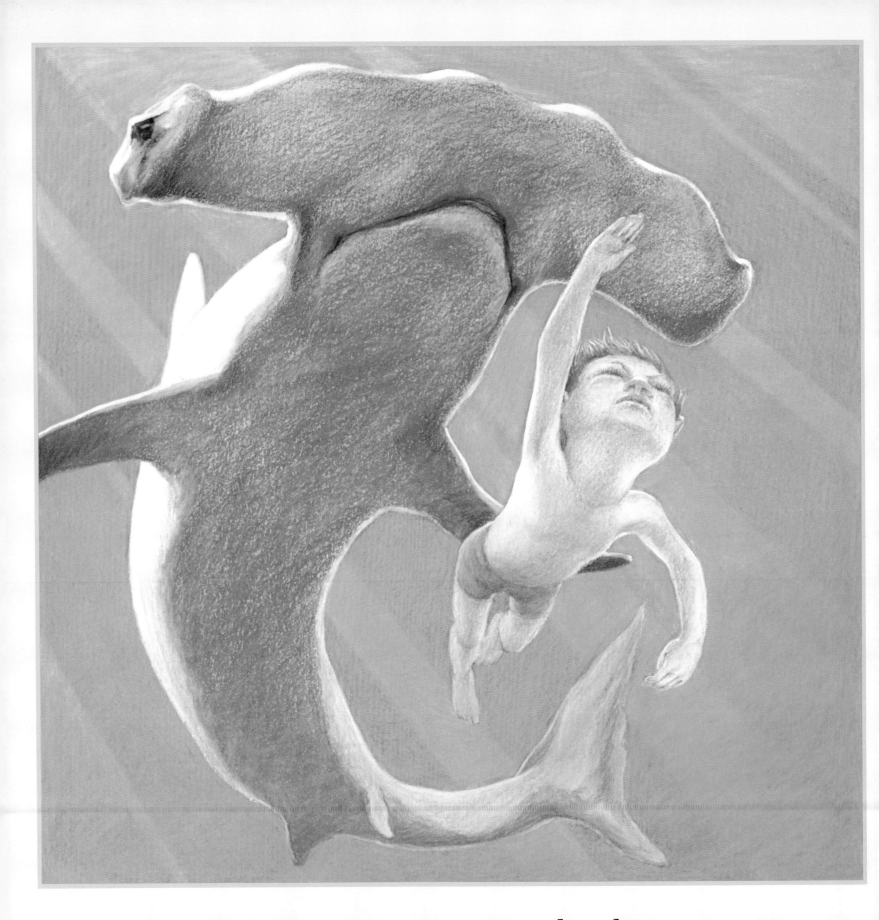

I'm as mean as a shark.

I'm as cold as a toad,

I'm as hot as a fox,

I'm as weak as a kitten,

I'm as strong as an ox.

I'm as loud as a lion,

I'm as quiet as a clam,

I'm as tough as a rhino,

I'm as gentle as a lamb.

I'm as brave as a tiger,

I'm as shy as a shrimp,

I'm as tame as a poodle,

I'm as wild as a chimp.

I'm as lazy as a lizard,

I'm as busy as a bee,

Put it all together,

And you've got ME!